# TAKEDOWN

*Also by Stephen Leather*

Pay Off
The Fireman
Hungry Ghost
The Chinaman
The Vets
The Long Shot
The Birthday Girl
The Double Tap
The Solitary Man
The Tunnel Rats
The Bombmaker
The Stretch
Tango One
The Eyewitness
First Response

*Spider Shepherd thrillers*
Hard Landing
Soft Target
Cold Kill
Hot Blood
Dead Men
Live Fire
Rough Justice
Fair Game
False Friends
True Colours
White Lies
Black Ops
Dark Forces

*Jack Nightingale supernatural thrillers*
Nightfall
Midnight
Nightmare
Nightshade
Lastnight